BOOK 1

HiLO

THE BOY WHO CRASHED TO EARTH

BY **JUDD WINICK**

WITH COLOR BY GUY MAJOR

RANDOM HOUSE 🏠 NEW YORK

Copyright © 2015 by Judd Winick
All rights reserved. Published in the United States by Random House Children's Books,
a division of Random House LLC, a Penguin Random House Company, New York.
Random House and the colophon are registered trademarks of Random House LLC.
Visit us on the Web! randomhousekids.com
Educators and librarians, for a variety of teaching tools, visit us at RHTeachersLibrarians.com
Library of Congress Cataloging-in-Publication Data
Winick, Judd.
The boy who crashed to Earth / Judd Winick. — First edition.
p. cm. — (Hilo ; book 1)
Summary: "When a mysterious boy falls from the sky, friends D.J. and Gina must discover
the secrets of his identity and help him save the world." —Provided by publisher.
ISBN 978-0-385-38617-3 (trade) — ISBN 978-0-385-38618-0 (lib. bdg.) — ISBN 978-0-385-38619-7 (ebook)
1. Graphic novels. [1. Graphic novels. 2. Amnesia—Fiction. 3. Identity—Fiction. 4. Robots—Fiction.
5. Extraterrestrial beings—Fiction. 6. Friendship—Fiction. 7. Science fiction.] I. Title.
PZ7.7.W57Boy 2015 [Fic]—dc23 2014030736
MANUFACTURED IN CHINA
10 9 8 7 6 5 4 3 2 1
Book design by John Sazaklis
First Edition

FOR
the
Catman

the
tUFF
Little
kitten

and

AAAAAAH!

2

3

AAAAHH!!

SCRAAAAACCK

CHAPTER 2

GOOD AT ONE THING

WHICH IS HARD IN MY FAMILY. THERE ARE **FIVE** OF US KIDS.

I HAVE TWO OLDER BROTHERS AND TWO YOUNGER SISTERS.

AND THEY ARE ALL **AWESOME** AT SOMETHING.

LOUIS PLAYS TENNIS.

17 YEARS OLD

DEXTER IS A WHIZ AT CHEMISTRY.

13 YEARS OLD

JENNIFER PLAYS VIOLIN. AND SINGS. **AND** DANCES BALLET.

9 YEARS OLD

AND LISA DOES **EVERYTHING** TWO YEARS EARLY. WALKING, TALKING, MATH, SWIMMING. SEVEN YEARS OLD AND ALREADY IN THE THIRD GRADE.

ME? I DON'T DO BETTER THAN OKAY IN EVERYTHING.

ME. 10 YEARS OLD.

EXCEPT **ONE** THING. THERE WAS JUST ONE THING I WAS GOOD AT.

GINA.

I WAS GOOD AT BEING FRIENDS WITH GINA.

SHE LIVED NEXT DOOR TO US SINCE I WAS TWO.

GINA!!

GIIIIINA!

CHECK IT OUT! **CHECK IT OUT!** MR. ANTONELLI HAD ANOTHER GARAGE SALE!

SERIOUSLY? HE HAS ONE EVERY WEEK. AND EVERYTHING SMELLS LIKE FEET.

YEAH, WELL, THIS IS **FOOT STINK FREE.** HE GAVE IT TO ME FOR A DOLLAR.

WHAT IS IT?

DON'T DIE. IT'S SO AWESOME, YOU MAY DIE.

WHAT IS IT?!

TUNK

AN ENTIRE BOX OF PLASTIC ELEPHANTS.

WHOA.

I KNOW.

WHOA.

I KNOW.

WHAT SHOULD WE DO WITH THEM?

FLYING ELEPHANTS!!

IT WAS COOL.

THEN...

WHEN WE WERE SEVEN YEARS OLD...

HER DAD GOT A NEW JOB. AND THEY MOVED AWAY.

RUA 1712

I WAS FRIENDS WITH GINA AND I WAS GOOD AT THAT.

SHE LEFT AND I WASN'T GOOD AT ANYTHING.

THREE YEARS LATER

BOOM

21

22

25

27

DO YOU LIVE HERE BY YOURSELF?

NO, I LIVE WITH MY FAMILY. BUT THEY'RE OUT.

OUT?

MY DAD IS WORKING LATE. MY MOM IS AT MY AUNT HELEN'S. MY OLDER BROTHER IS AT TENNIS PRACTICE. MY **OTHER** BROTHER IS AT SCIENCE CLUB. MY LITTLE SISTER IS AT BALLET REHEARSAL. AND MY OTHER LITTLE SISTER IS AT A PIANO LESSON.

I DON'T DO ANYTHING. SO I'M HERE.

I WOULDN'T SAY YOU DON'T DO **ANYTHING.** I FELL FROM THE SKY AND YOU GAVE ME RICE AND MILK.

I THINK THAT'S COOLER THAN WHATEVER TENNIS PRACTICE IS.

SNIFF

BUT BALLET REHEARSAL SOUNDS NEAT.

CAN YOU EAT THESE? BECAUSE THEY SMELL **AWFUL.**

35

WHUMP

ZZZZ
ZZZ

IS THIS YOUR LABORATORY?

37

38

39

41

43

HILO?

YOU SHOVED ME INTO A CLOSET.

YEAH. SORRY. I COULDN'T LET MY BROTHER SEE YOU.

WHY? DID HE THINK I TOUCHED HIS GUITAR?

LISTEN ... NO ONE CAN SEE YOU. AT LEAST NOT UNTIL WE FIGURE OUT SOME MORE STUFF ABOUT YOU.

BUT I WANT TO GO TO SCHOOL.

YOU CAN'T. YOU AREN'T -- WHAT DO THEY CALL IT? **ENROLLED?**

I WANT TO GO WITH YOU.

IT'LL BE OKAY. YOU'LL HAVE THE WHOLE HOUSE TO YOURSELF.

WHAT ABOUT **RAZORWARK?**

WHO?

RAZORWARK.

DO YOU KNOW WHO THAT IS?

NO.

I DON'T EITHER. SORRY. I **SHOULD** KNOW WHO HE IS. BUT MY MEMORY IS FULL OF HOLES. BUSTED BOOK.

WHEN I WAS SLEEPING, I REMEMBERED SOMETHING ABOUT HIM. NOW I DON'T KNOW WHAT IT WAS....

GINA

STUDENTS, SAY HELLO TO --

GINA COOPER. OUR FIRST NEW STUDENT TODAY ...

I UNDERSTAND THAT YOU WERE ORIGINALLY FROM OUR TOWN, BUT YOU MOVED AWAY A FEW YEARS AGO?

YES. WE MOVED TO NEW YORK, BUT MY DAD GOT A NEW JOB BACK HERE IN BERKE COUNTY.

MY OLD HOUSE WAS NEXT TO D.J.'S.

IS IT NICE TO BE BACK?

KIND OF. I MISS MY FRIENDS BACK IN NEW YORK.

BUT EVERYTHING HERE SEEMS THE SAME, JUST SMALLER.

THAT'S BECAUSE YOU WERE SMALLER WHEN YOU WERE LAST HERE, SO EVERYTHING APPEARED BIGGER.

UH, YES. WELL, OUR OTHER NEW STUDENT IS HILO --

AAAHH!

I LOVE THAT GREETING.

I SEE. AND, UM, WHERE DID YOU LIVE BEFORE YOU MOVED HERE?

UH-OH.

WE DON'T KNOW. WE THINK OUTER SPACE. D.J. FOUND ME AFTER I FELL FROM THE SKY.

OH NO.

HILO, WE DON'T HAVE THIS KIND OF MISCHIEF IN MY CLASS.

OKAY.

WHAT KIND OF MISCHIEF **DO** YOU HAVE?

I SEE FROM YOUR FILE THAT YOU LIVED IN **DALLAS.**

YES! DALLAS! THE THIRD-LARGEST CITY IN TEXAS AND THE NINTH-LARGEST IN THE UNITED STATES!

DIVIDED AMONG COLLIN, DALLAS, DENTON, KAUFMAN, AND ROCKWALL COUNTIES, THE CITY HAS A POPULATION OF 1,300,350.

DUDE. YOUR PAL IS A REAL FREAK.

ANNUAL RAINFALL IS 40.9 INCHES.

57

SO, HILO. YOU ACTUALLY FELL FROM THE SKY?

YEAH! I WAS JUST WEARING SILVER UNDERPANTS. I **REALLY** LIKE THEM, BUT D.J. SAID I CAN'T WALK AROUND IN THEM. NOW THAT I'M OUT AND ABOUT, I CAN SEE THAT NOBODY IS WEARING SILVER UNDERPANTS.

YOU'RE FUNNY.

YEAH! HEH! HE JUST NEVER STOPS, Y'KNOW, JOKING AROUND.

WELL, I LIVE DOWN THIS WAY ON ELM. HILO, DO YOU LIVE NEAR D.J.'S HOUSE?

I LIVE **IN** D.J.'S HOUSE. BUT DON'T TELL HIS FAMILY. THEY AREN'T SUPPOSED TO KNOW.

HA! **SEE?!** ALWAYS JOKING!

BUT, UM, GINA...MAYBE YOU COULD COME OVER LATER. OR I COULD COME OVER TO YOUR NEW HOUSE OR SOMETHING.

WE COULD HANG OUT.

LIKE WE USED TO.

OH, I'D LIKE THAT, BUT I CAN'T.

I...I HAVE TO GO HOME AND PRACTICE.

PRACTICE? PRACTICE FOR WHAT?

GINA'S HOUSE.

HEY, HEY! IT'S TIME TO FIGHT!

EVERYBODY YELL "BLUE AND WHITE!"

HEY, HEY! LET'S DO IT AGAIN! EVERYBODY YELL "GO! FIGHT! WIN!"

61

DAD, WHERE ARE YOU GOING?

I'VE GOT TO HEAD BACK TO THE OFFICE. THE LAB IS BARELY SET UP.

BOOP

BUT YOU SAID YOU'D HELP ME PUT MY TELESCOPE TOGETHER.

I CAN'T, KIDDO. IT'LL HAVE TO WAIT.

BUT THERE'S THAT METEOR SHOWER TONIGHT. NASA DIDN'T EVEN KNOW ABOUT IT UNTIL LAST NIGHT! DO YOU KNOW HOW **RARE** THAT IS?

I'M SO SORRY, GINA. I AM. BUT I REALLY HAVE TO GO. I'LL SEE YOU LATER.

CLIK

SO YOU STILL LIKE ASTRONOMY?

ASTRONOMY: THE BRANCH OF SCIENCE THAT DEALS WITH CELESTIAL OBJECTS, SPACE, AND THE PHYSICAL UNIVERSE AS A WHOLE.

YEAH. BACK AT MY OLD SCHOOL IN NEW YORK, OUR ASTRONOMY CLUB WOULD GO TO THE PLANETARIUM AND USE THE REAL BIG TELESCOPE.

WE DON'T HAVE A PLANETARIUM. OR AN ASTRONOMY CLUB.

OR A SCIENCE CLUB. OR A BOOK CLUB. OR MATHLETES.

I GOT OUT OF HAVING TO JOIN CHEERLEADING WITH MY SISTERS BECAUSE I WAS SO BUSY WITH MY OTHER STUFF.

MY MOM WANTS ME TO BE JUST LIKE MY SISTERS. ALL THEY DO IS TALK ABOUT BOYS AND CLOTHES.

WHAT DO YOU WANT?

I WANT TO GO HOME.

64

EXCEPT THESE. YOU DON'T NEED THEM.

DO **NOT** EAT THOSE.

WHY?

IT USUALLY TAKES ME AND MY DAD AN HOUR TO PUT THIS TOGETHER. AND HE'S AN ENGINEER.

YEAH! WELL, UM, I GUESS THIS WILL KEEP YOU BUSY! MAYBE YOU WON'T HAVE TO BE A CHEERLEADER!

NO. MY MOM WON'T LET ME PLAY SOCCER UNLESS I CHEER.

YOU PLAY SOCCER NOW TOO?

YEAH. WELL, BACK HOME IN NEW YORK I DID. DO YOU PLAY ANY SPORTS?

NO.

I DON'T PLAY ANYTHING.

BUT D.J. THINKS BALLET SOUNDS PRETTY COOL.

WHAT?! NO! **YOU** SAID THAT! I DIDN'T--

AND D.J. FED ME RICE AND MILK **AND** GAVE ME THESE CLOTHES SO I'M NOT WALKING AROUND IN THE PREVIOUSLY MENTIONED SILVER UNDERPANTS.

YOU **REALLY** LIKE THOSE SILVER UNDERPANTS.

THEY ARE OUTSTANDING! DO YOU WANT TO SEE THEM?

HEY!

HA! AND I THOUGHT MOVING BACK HERE WOULD BE TOTALLY BORING.

BORING?

WELL, YEAH. THIS IS BERKE COUNTY. NOTHING NEW EVER HAPPENS HERE.

CHAPTER

5

NOTHING NEW EVER HAPPENS HERE

munch
munch

69

HILO?

HILO!

MAYBE HE HAD TO GO TO THE BATHROOM. HE COULD HAVE JUST HAVE USED OURS.

I NEED TO -- I HAVE TO --

I HAVE TO GO AFTER HIM.

HILO?!

HILO!

OVER HERE.

WHAT ARE YOU DOING? WHY -- **WHOA!**

WHAT IS THAT?

IT'S A BIG HOLE.

I SEE THAT. BUT IT LOOKS JUST LIKE --

THE HOLE I MADE WHEN I CRASHED TO EARTH.

YEAH. MAYBE THERE'S ANOTHER DUDE LIKE YOU.

NO.

IT'S BECAUSE YOU **REALLY** FELL FROM THE SKY.

D.J., YOU DROPPED YOUR BAG.

THANKS.

HILO...WHERE... WHERE **ARE** YOU FROM?

I DON'T REMEMBER.

CLACK

CLACK

CRACK

84

WHAT ABOUT HILO?
IS HE -- IS HE OKAY?

NOT EXACTLY.

CHAPTER

DIG

89

WOW.

I KNOW!

ALL THE PIECES FIT!

SO YOU'RE A ROBOT. MAYBE YOU'RE NOT FROM SPACE. MAYBE YOU **ARE** A GOVERNMENT EXPERIMENT. MAYBE YOU ESCAPED AND THEY SENT THE RANT AFTER YOU.

I HAD A DREAM, BUT IT WASN'T A DREAM. IT WAS A MEMORY.

I WAS FIGHTING... SOMEONE.

RAZORWARK?

YES.

I WAS FIGHTING HIM. WE WERE ON OUR WORLD... THEN I FELL THROUGH A HOLE.

AND I LANDED HERE.

MAYBE HE'S FROM ANOTHER DIMENSION. LIKE IN THE NARNIA BOOKS. OR AN ALTERNATE REALITY LIKE IN COMICS.

YOU STILL READ COMICS?

YEAH.

COOL.

HILO, DO YOU REMEMBER **WHY** YOU WERE FIGHTING RAZORWARK?

COULD BE AN OCTOPED! THEN WE'VE GOT **SEVEN** MORE FEET TO FIND.

OCTOPED! I **SO** WANTED TO USE THAT WORD IN A SENTENCE TODAY, AND **BOOM!**

OCTOPED!

OKAY, OKAY, BUT NOW WHAT? WE CAN'T JUST LEAVE IT HERE.

NO. WE HAVE TO PUT IT IN YOUR ROOM.

NO.

YOUR ROOM?

NO.

WELL, IT'S GOTTA GO IN SOMEBODY'S ROOM.

WAIT, I KNOW! I GOT A ROOM! THE CLUBHOUSE!

THIS IS **GREAT!** AND NOT JUST BECAUSE IT PERFECTLY FITS A GIANT METAL FOOT AND SMELLS LIKE SQUIRREL POOP. IT'S 'CAUSE IT'S OVERRUN WITH A **TON** OF SPIDERS.

OCTOPEDS.

OCTOPEDS!

HELLO, MY EIGHT-LEGGED BROTHERS!

WE'RE LUCKY OUR OLD CLUBHOUSE IS STILL HERE.

NAH. IT'LL NEVER FALL DOWN.

YEAH, YOU'RE RIGHT. NOTHING EVER CHANGES IN BERKE COUNTY.

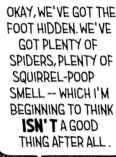

OKAY, WE'VE GOT THE FOOT HIDDEN. WE'VE GOT PLENTY OF SPIDERS, PLENTY OF SQUIRREL-POOP SMELL -- WHICH I'M BEGINNING TO THINK **ISN'T** A GOOD THING AFTER ALL.

BUT NOW ALL WE HAVE TO DO IS WAIT.

AND LISTEN.

LISTEN?

THWACK

SORRY. NOT LISTEN. **FEEL.**

AND NOT **WE.**

JUST ME.

I FEEL.

FEEL FOR WHAT?

OTHERS.

OTHERS LIKE THE RANT. THEY'LL WANT THE FOOT. OR **OTHER** FEET. I'LL FEEL 'EM WHEN THEY SHOW UP.

I DON'T KNOW HOW I KNOW. I JUST KNOW. BUSTED BOOK MEMORY.

C'MON!

YOU FEEL A RANT COMING?!

NO! IT'S ALMOST DINNERTIME! LET'S GO TO D.J.'S HOUSE!

I THOUGHT YOU WERE WAITING FOR YOUR "FEELINGS"?!

I CAN DO **THAT** ANYWHERE! BUT DINNER AT **YOUR** HOUSE CAN ONLY BE AT YOUR HOUSE!

DO WE HAVE TO?! I'D MUCH RATHER BE ATTACKED BY A GIANT ROBOT INSECT!

I REALLY WOULD.

107

109

TEXAS. HE'S FROM TEXAS!

IT'S THE CORE OF THE LARGEST INLAND METROPOLITAN AREA IN THE UNITED STATES THAT LACKS ANY NAVIGABLE LINK TO THE SEA.

YOU DON'T HAVE AN ACCENT.

SHOULD I?

MOST PEOPLE FROM TEXAS HAVE AN ACCENT. WERE YOU BORN THERE?

I DON'T THINK SO. I FELL FROM THE SKY.

HA HA HA HA! HILO'S ALWAYS MAKING JOKES.

HE WASN'T JOKING. HE SAID HE FELL FROM THE SKY. **TWICE.**

THIS IS **BAD.** LISA IS THE SMARTEST ONE HERE. AND THE ONLY ONE WHO REALLY PAYS ATTENTION. HILO'S GOTTA ACT NORMAL.

HILO IS EATING HIS NAPKIN.

112

EXCUSE ME?

I DO NOT.

IT'S BECKY DAHLMAN.

TOTALLY BECKY DAHLMAN.

WHO'S BECKY DAHLMAN?

LOUIS'S GIRLFRIEND.

IT'S **NOT** BECKY DAHLMAN!

BUT YOU **DO** HAVE A GIRLFRIEND...

GO, GO, GO.

THANK YOU FOR DINNER!

THAT WAS GREAT! WE SHOULD HAVE DINNER AGAIN RIGHT NOW! YOUR FAMILY IS OUTSTANDING!

I'M GLAD SOMEONE THINKS SO.

YOU DON'T LIKE YOUR FAMILY?

OF COURSE I DO. I JUST DON'T LIKE LIVING WITH THEM SOMETIMES.

WHY DON'T YOU LEAVE?

WHAT? WHAT DO YOU MEAN?

IF YOU DON'T LIKE IT HERE, YOU COULD GO. MOVE.

VACATE : *VERB.* TO CEASE TO OCCUPY OR HOLD ; GIVE UP.

ABBOT

HILO... I'M NOT GOING TO **RUN AWAY.**

WHY?

LOTS OF REASONS. BUT MOSTLY ... BECAUSE IT WOULDN'T **FIX** ANYTHING .

DO YOU UNDERSTAND?

YOU LOOK CONFUSED.

NO...IT'S NOT THAT.

IT'S...

BURP!

HA HA HA HA!

REPEAT BUSINESS!

WHY DO BOYS ALWAYS LAUGH AT BURPING?

HILO!

HANG ON! HANG ON! IT'S OKAY! IT HAPPENED BEFORE!

YES. STILL BREATHING. STILL PUMPING.

HE'S ASLEEP.

ZZZZ
ZZZZ
ZZ ZZZ

WOW. IT'S A GOOD THING HE DIDN'T PASS OUT IN FRONT OF YOUR FAMILY. THAT WOULD HAVE BEEN HARD TO EXPLAIN.

YEAH.

BUT THEY PROBABLY WOULD HAVE BEEN TOO BUSY TO NOTICE.

HA!

YEAH, THEY DO HAVE A LOT GOING ON.

BUT THEY AREN'T **SO** BAD ... ARE THEY?

NO.

THEY'RE A LOT LIKE YOU, ACTUALLY.

WHAT?

THEY'RE ALL GOOD AT A BUNCH OF STUFF.

LIKE YOU.

BUT NOT ME.

I'M PRETTY BORING.

YOU'RE NOT BORING.

I AM.

I KNOW THE ONLY REASON YOU'RE HANGING OUT WITH ME IS BECAUSE OF HILO.

HE SURE ISN'T BORING.

D.J., THAT'S NOT TRUE. I --

WE USED TO BE FRIENDS. THEN YOU MOVED AWAY. AND ...

YOU CHANGED.

BUT THAT'S OKAY. YOU'RE SUPPOSED TO CHANGE.

BUT I DIDN'T.

I'M JUST LIKE THE CLUBHOUSE.

AND BERKE COUNTY.

I'M THE SAME.

I'M **ALWAYS** GOING TO BE THE SAME.

D.J....

YOU SHOULD GO. YOUR PARENTS ARE GOING TO WONDER WHERE YOU ARE. AND YOU'RE GOING TO MISS THE METEOR SHOWER.

I NEED TO STAY WITH HILO.

I'LL SEE YOU TOMORROW.

CLICK

118

CHAPTER

7

RUN

YOU WILL
FAIL, HILO.

124

OKAY?!

OKAY.

BUT YOU ARE REALLY SLOW!

I AM NOT.

BE QUIET AND RUN!

OUR FRIEND NEEDS US.

135

139

140

CHAPTER

I STOP THEM WHEN THEY GO WRONG

IT'S CALLED AN OBLITERATRON.

IS THAT BAD?

YES. OBLITERATRONS ONLY DO **ONE** THING. THEY DESTROY WORLDS.

AND ...

I REMEMBER.

THEY SERVE **RAZORWARK.**

OBLITERATRONS ARE TOO BIG TO TRAVEL. HE TELEPORTS THEM IN PIECES. THEN HE SENDS THE BUGS TO PUT THEM TOGETHER.

THIS IS MY FAULT.

RAZORWARK SENT THEM THROUGH THE HOLE I CAME OUT OF.

THE MONSTER I DREAMT I WAS FIGHTING...

RAZORWARK.

HE'S THE MOST POWERFUL ROBOT ON OUR WORLD.

HE DOESN'T BELIEVE MACHINES SHOULD SERVE **ANYONE** ANYMORE.

HE'S LEADING A WAR AGAINST ALL LIVING THINGS.

HE LAUNCHED HIS BIGGEST... HIS MOST DEVASTATING ATTACK ON **FARALON.**

WHAT'S FARALON?

YOU WERE SCARED.

THAT'S OKAY.

BUT RUNNING AWAY DIDN'T FIX ANYTHING, DID IT?

AND NOW HE'S SENT THE OBLITERATRON TO DESTROY YOUR WORLD.

I CAN'T BE SCARED. I CAN'T RUN AWAY.

AND I DON'T LET **ANYONE** HURT MY FRIENDS.

C'MON. WE GOTTA GET DOWN THERE!

AND DO **WHAT?**

BEAT ON SOME BUGS!

A **THOUSAND** OF THEM?!

HILO NEEDS US!

OKAY! BUT WE'RE NOT JUST GOING TO DIVE INTO A HALF TON OF ANGRY ROBOTIC INSECTS! WE NEED A PLAN!

RUN.

THAT'S YOUR PLAN?

D.J.! HIS **MOUTH!** LIKE HILO DID! GO FOR ITS —

CHUNK

FLOP

URK

BUUUUUUUURP

CHUNG

HE ... HE WANTS YOU TO DESTROY THIS ENTIRE WORLD ... JUST TO GET TO **ME?**

TO GET TO YOU ...

RAZORWARK WOULD LAY WASTE TO **HUNDREDS** OF PLANETS.

YOU SHOULD NEVER HAVE RUN, HILO.

TZAACK

166

CRACK

HILO!

OW.

HANG ON! I'VE GOT YOU!

I...CAN'T HURT HIM.

IF I CAN'T HURT HIM, I CAN'T STOP HIM.

177

182

CHAPTER

GONE

I WAS GOING TO LEAVE AN **EAR**, BUT THAT'S GROSS TOO AND I REALLY NEED MY EARS. BUT ANYWAY --

I HAD TO LEAVE A BIT OF ME BEHIND.

WHY?

IN CASE I NEEDED TO TALK TO YOU.

SOMETHING TERRIBLE HAS HAPPENED.

I NEED YOUR HELP.

WHAT DO I HAVE TO DO?

YOU HAVE TO GO. **NOW.** GET GINA.

191

END OF BOOK ONE

JUDD WINICK grew up on Long Island, where he spent countless hours doodling, reading **X-Men** comics and the newspaper strip **Bloom County**, and watching **Looney Tunes**. Today Judd lives in San Francisco with his wife, Pam Ling; their two kids; and their cats, Chaka and Sleestak. When Judd isn't collecting far more action figures and vinyl toys than a normal adult, he is a screenwriter and an award-winning cartoonist. Judd has scripted issues of bestselling comics series, including Batman, Green Lantern, Green Arrow, Justice League, and Star Wars. Judd also appeared as a cast member of MTV's **The Real World: San Francisco** and is the author of the highly acclaimed graphic novel **Pedro and Me**, about his **Real World** cast-mate and friend, AIDS activist Pedro Zamora. Visit Judd and Hilo online at **juddwinick.com**.

DON'T MISS THE NEXT ADVENTURE

SAVING THE WHOLE WIDE WORLD

COMING TO A PLANET
NEAR YOU IN 2016!

SAVING THE WORLD HAS NEVER BEEN SO FUN!